# Unspoken Verses

Irin Anna Cherian

**Ukiyoto Publishing**

All global publishing rights are held by

**Ukiyoto Publishing**

Published in 2024

Content Copyright © Irin Anna Cherian
ISBN 9789367951354

*All rights reserved.*

*No part of this publication may be reproduced, transmitted, or stored in a retrieval system, in any form by any means, electronic, mechanical, photocopying, recording or otherwise, without the prior permission of the publisher.*

*The moral rights of the author have been asserted.*

*This is a work of fiction. Names, characters, businesses, places, events, locales, and incidents are either the products of the author's imagination or used in a fictitious manner. Any resemblance to actual persons, living or dead, or actual events is purely coincidental.*

This book is sold subject to the condition that it shall not by way of trade or otherwise, be lent, resold, hired out or otherwise circulated, without the publisher's prior consent, in any form of binding or cover other than that in which it is published.

www.ukiyoto.com

*To Devu and Ashna*

# Contents

| | |
|---|---|
| Grudge | 1 |
| To Be A Person | 2 |
| Where are we today? | 4 |
| Muted Memories | 6 |
| For You | 7 |
| Not Today | 8 |
| Tired | 9 |
| Untouched, Unseen, Unheard | 10 |
| Nothing But A Woman | 11 |
| Crimson Red | 12 |
| What Love You Have Left | 13 |
| Dear Mama | 15 |
| Let It Flow | 17 |
| I'm sorry, Antappa... | 18 |
| Glass Room | 19 |
| I Started Something I Couldn't Complete | 21 |
| Dear Ones | 22 |
| Overripe Peaches | 23 |
| Graveyard of our Conversations | 24 |
| Dear Poem | 25 |
| Kings and Kingfisher | 26 |
| Was it today? | 27 |
| Let Go | 28 |
| Runaway | 29 |
| How Much I Hate You | 31 |
| Not Meant To Be | 33 |
| Who Am I | 35 |

| | |
|---|---|
| Eulogy | 36 |
| Where does it go? | 37 |
| The Lady Next Door | 38 |
| | |
| *About the Author* | *39* |

# Grudge

Hold me like a grudge,

Inside the depth of your mind. Hold me like a regret,

Keep thinking about me in and out.

Inside the mansion of your mind,

I wanna survive like a rotten piece of flesh – So rotten that you cannot take the smell,

That you cannot stop thinking about me,

That you cannot ignore me,

I want to live inside you

Like rotten pieces or red roses, I don't care!

I want to wrap you around in your own blood

I want you to hold me close till your breath knows no more!

This is the love I carry for you,

Carried it all along my life,

Love rot to become an obsession – Obsession fought hard to be limerence

I want to smell your sweat, your blood,

On the face of the absurd, I covered my face in wrath! I waited for you at the end of the world

Tell me, darling, if this is not love… what is?

# To Be A Person

What does it take to be a person? Eyes, nose, flesh, and bones,
Mind, body, brain, and hope for the future?

When I can't get out of bed,
When every day, I pray to god for death,
Would you still call me a person?

When I cut my right shoulder and left thigh, And love to see the blood flowing out of them…
Would you still call me a person?

When I want to jump out
of every bridge that I pass by,
Would you still call me a person?

Each time I wake up wanting to take my life, I wonder what kind of a person I am!
Then I realize I'm barely a person.

I'm a sack of flesh and bone with no will to live. I'm barely human,
I run around pretending to be one.

Maybe if I pretend long enough I can become a person!
I want to roll around these thorns
and make myself bleed heavily and die out of it.

I know it's odd; I know it's dark But as I said, I'm barely a person!

# Where are we today?

Where are we today?

I am brewing black coffee

You can smell it from our balcony Our legs leaned against the walls Making dirty footprints on the wall

I pour a drop or two of coffee on your lips and slowly kiss you Tasting the black coffee from your lips

Your lips; the favorite residing place of my lips.

Where are we today?

Today we are walking down the beach The waves are slowly touching our bodies

You talk about how you started loving the beach after "we" happened... We lay down on the beach, for the salty water to cover us

We hold our hands and when we walk we carry the pieces of the beach along with us We walk to the lighthouse, with our bodies covered in sand

Panting, our eyes met

Slowly leaning forward to kiss you, tasting the saltiness in your mouth I want to rest my head on your chest and talk about the universe.

Where are we today?

We are in the right corner of the library,

walking between the agony and pain of poets and writers

I am searching for Dostoevsky; you touch me from behind and kiss my neck I always wanted this, from the time I was a little girl,

I wanted to get fucked while Kafka and Camus stare at me,

telling it's all meaningless!
While I find meaning in you,
For a millisecond, you, my darling is, meaning.

Where are we today?
The swimming pool of a five-star hotel In a sleeper bus with curtains closed
In the forest in the middle of the night
In your room while your parents are asleep

I don't know you, I've never met you,
But I've traveled places with you, and I am homesick… Homesick for all the places I've never been
Places we ought to be
Places that only remain in our collective imagination. You know what?
The places I've never been with you are my favorite places.

# Muted Memories

I remember days, days that passed by just like that. Then some memories flaunt through your mind.

The day I lost my watercolor, The day my dog died,
The day I helped an old woman cross the road.

Then there are others,
Muted, living deep inside you, Forgotten, you shut them down.

The day my grandfather died,
The day my teacher touched my breasts, The day my dad beat my mom,

Muted memories,
I feel nothing for them.

But I stare at the ceiling and wonder about them all day long, Muted memories….

Memories I want to erase out of my head. Memories that don't worry me, don't hurt me,
Or maybe I'm just well-adjusted to the pain it inflicts.

# For You

I wrote this poem for you,

Carefully carved every word out of the love I feel for you. You're my sunset and sunrise; I want to stare at you forever. I wanna kiss your dry lips and make them wet.

I can look at you from dusk till dawn, every day, every night until this universe explodes. You're the best qualia I ever had, not the night sky or waterfalls.

You know when I need a hug, You know, when I want to cry, Like the wind, you softly

You softly touch my curls.

Like the stream, you gently wash away my scars.

Darling, let me lie on your shoulder and watch this sunset forever...

# Not Today

I was eight when I started hating myself

I hated the way my hair looked

I hated the way my body was

Maybe it was the shouting and the noises that made me who I am, Reckless and unworthy.

I starved myself at sixteen, to die out of rage at myself

Maybe it was the unwanted touches that made me who I am, Unenthusiastic and pathetic.

Pain flows through my veins, Hate pumps through my heart.

All I know is, I hate this life.

I was twenty when I slit my veins. I didn't know why I wanted to die.

Blood mixed with water across the bathroom floor

And my heart sang, "no more days, no more nights".

Someday, maybe I'll love myself.

Maybe I will love the curls that stand against the force of gravity,

  The round cheeks and the painful heart.

Someday, maybe I'll wake up with hope for the future, Make a cup of black coffee and wonder about the universe. Turn to the sea and adore a sunset

Maybe someday I'll love myself... But not today.

# Tired

I am tired to write today, More tired than yesterday.

Even more than the day before that I am growing tired,

I feel like ninety, Ninety and tired of life.

But I'm barely twenty-three....

This life scares me

Time scares me

The morning sky sometimes does too I am crying for things I don't know

I am mourning for the dead I never buried

All I know is that this tiredness is clutching my bones

My ligaments are about to break,

My veins are almost dry I have hatred for this life

Hatred towards for everyone and everything

## Untouched, Unseen, Unheard

I'm searching for you in places untouched, unseen, and unheard But you're nowhere to be found

You, the real you, have been missing for a while. How long will you hide?

How long will you seek the unseekable?

On the days I see these bougainvillea flowers

I think about you, about all the promises you made. It hurts, but you're nothing but a memory now.

I want to touch you; I want to run my fingers through your hair. I want to see the beaches and mountains with you.

Where are you hiding?

Within your dreams and delusions, you live

I'm searching for you; I've been searching for you forever. I ran to places we have been to,

The places untouched, unseen, and unheard. But you're nowhere to be found!

This reminds me of the time we used to play hide and seek I'm counting till infinity but you're not here

Were you ever here? Or was it always just me?

You're nothing but a memory now.

# Nothing But A Woman

Blood pouring down my nostrils like a valley of hatred
I am nothing but a woman
The rage of it drops down on my skin
It sticks to my skin like no other
I try to scrub it out, but it ain't going anywhere
I built these walls of anger out of the pain
 I had Out of the times my legs were clenched and
Spread wide open so men can go inside as they please
I want to be fire and burn them all
I want to be water and drown them all.
Charades of men poured through my life.
 Some abused, some loved.
I am as stubborn as I can be 'Cause these seasons made me so
The spring, the autumn, and the winter
My skin thickened by the hate you carry for me.

But I don't care about it I'm a woman, I'm 23
I don't need anything other than that to live
I waltz out like a woman, exceptional
A confident one
The one my daddy and mommy, taught me to be!

# Crimson Red

My body was covered in your blood, crimson red

The oranges we plucked from the orchard are still not ripe. The wine bottle you left half open is still waiting there.

The scars you carved on my body are not visible

But they lie on the inside, bleeding

The way you touched me still makes me feel suffocated

 I wanted to run away somewhere

But in the end, when you ripped me open, I couldn't take it anymore I was not afraid of the yelling

I was afraid of you... The whole of you...

Your red eyes and big beard

When I carved a knife through your heart I never thought it would be easy

But it was the easiest goodbye I ever said!

# What Love You Have Left

Your love; handwritten letters and soft kisses..

My delusions and my madness

My lethargy and my pessimism

How did you take it?

How did you take me in your arms softly and love me?

How did you kiss my neck and make me laugh till my stomach hurt?

I was never enough,

Never enough for anyone.


I was made of pain and sins,

You loved me like it was the end of the world; I lied;

I lied about being happy when I was sad, I lied about taking therapy

As I wandered, lost in books that nearly devoured me I lied about taking care of myself

when I carved scars on my body

How can you love me so much when I clearly hate myself? I want to learn love from you

Learn the way you love a dying thing

The flower you kept in the middle of that book

The butterfly you still weep for and among all dying things, me…


Did you ever regret all the love you gave? Or you just kept loving, just like that?

Darling… Did you spend all your love on me, this sick monster? Darling, do you have any love left?

I know it's not fair.

But even in my death bed,
I would need your love to die peacefully.

# Dear Mama

Mama I want to say that I love you,

I want to knock on your door, but panic is all I can feel.

My heart is beating like it's the end of it

My body is shivering, Feels like I'm dying,

But that was all I ever wanted.


Why am I afraid?

Mama, I have once tried to choke myself to death I cut myself and bled an ocean of pain

Mama, I'm tired– Tired of waking up

Tired of even brushing my teeth

When I pass through these bridges, All I can think about is jumping.

Why did I grow up to be this mama?

You never taught me any of this…

 Instead, you taught me how to love

How to think about it all from another person's eyes

 You told me that sometimes it's okay to fail

But is it okay maa if I'm failing continuously? That all I am is a big failure

How am I never the daughter you raised me to be!


Mama, I love you!

But I don't think love is enough to cure this sickness Mama…

Deep inside, I don't want to die;

I want to lie down on your lap, talk about my day and listen to your lullaby

Every day when I wake up, all I can think about is how you will feel when I do what I want to do It sickens me, but the pain is too much

I have heard you say that, "Depression is for the weak." Sorry ma, I grew up to be weak and fragile..


Mama, I'm gonna knock on this door and tell you I need help. I have only two options, live or die

I want you to choose it for me

All I want is a lullaby and a small space on your lap, All I want is the help I deserve,

All I want is relief from all these pains. When I tell you, I need help..

Hug me and whisper in my ears, "Baby, it's gonna be alright." Or will you curse me for being what I am?

You once said, "It's all going to be alright..." Will you say it again?

Will you lift your arms and take me in it?

Mama... I am sick, and I need help.

# Let It Flow

It's snowing outside, and you need warmth
I need your body sliding mine
I need your lips to meet mine
I want you to stand behind me,
bite my ears and whisper, "I love you in every possible way."
I want to read poetry with my head on your lap
My curls touching your thighs.
I want to write stories staring at you
I want to see you naked and raw
I want to hug you and kiss your forehead.
I want you to run your hands through my stretch marks
I want to slide my fingers through your imperfect curves
I want us to be two lost souls making coffee and wondering about life.
Darling, I know what we have is complicated
But I don't want us to think…
I want you to close your eyes and just let it be
Let it flow till it flows
When our streams get dry,
we can go mad in nostalgia of our old lives.

## I'm sorry, Antappa...

What did it take you to do it? I wanted to ask

How did you do it?

Where did you get the courage?

You were 10,

10 which you could count with your fingers

Still the fear lingers

I am very sorry

I wish you found Whatever you were looking for – Love or peace, whatever it was

People think you were a kid Hence nothing is justified.

But I see it–

Your pain, for 10 minutes or 10 years

Your impulsivity, for 10 minutes or 10 years

It was enough...

I am sorry for all the pain you felt. If you can hear this

I'm sure you can't, but wouldn't it be nice?

I hope you found what you were looking for – And if you regret it, let's swap positions Because I'm sure I won't regret.

I don't know who you're

But why is it that I miss you?

# Glass Room

I'll lock you inside this glass room
Give you Plath's poetry and a bottle of red wine
I whisper in your ears, "I have a surprise."
But you don't listen –
You don't listen a lot these days You don't remember a lot
The memories which we owned are just mine now.

Air is pumped out of the glass room You feel suffocated now
Choking for real,
But you were, all these years!

Things are blurry
But you're smiling at me Even if you're dying
You're still loving me even if I'm killing you
 I want to kill you to stop hurting… to stop loving…
Because our love darling is bleeding today.

Things are blurry
As you take your last breaths
I remember you saying how you wanted to suffocate and die
To finally undo the basic human nature of breathing back.

When you take your last breath, I watch you from another glass room,
half drowned You remember? You don't these days

Is it paranoia? Is it madness?
I don't imagine things I do it
Is it me who forgets and you who remember?
You wanted to suffocate, don't blame me now!

I want to save you I want to drown
I want to save us
I took it as a punishment A last scar, the last pain
I want to see you close your eyes forever.
I want to see your scars stop bleeding.
I see you die
The last thing I'll ever see My last pain, my love
The water that covers me is now full of love, Or is it pain?
Was our love a synonym for pain all along?

# I Started Something I Couldn't Complete

I want to call myself a reader,
But the unfinished books stare at me all day long;
 I would start reading but couldn't complete....

I want to call myself a lover,
But looking at you, I know that's not just.
I started loving you, but Couldn't complete.

I want to call myself an artist,
But the unwritten book tightens its arms around my neck.
Blank pages grasp a story's hold on my throat.

I am a half-written poem, An unfinished work of art, A broken piece of mirror, A journey you started,
But never finished.

Running in loops Evading everything Trying to get to the end
Trying to scream but hyperventilating

But in the middle, I always get tired. Just like the book I left unread,
Just like the kiss we didn't finish
 Just like a million other things....

# Dear Ones

Dear Amma and Appa,

I wish I could be the daughter you wished to be, Instead, I became the prodigal one.

Dear brother,

I wouldn't have known this world this well without you.

Dear casual lover,

I like you too much to break your heart. I wish it would hurt less when things end.

Dear ex-best friend

On the way, we lost each other; In between, I lost myself.

Dear Abuser,

I've not healed enough to forgive you, And I don't think you deserve it either.

Dear best friend,

I will bleed to death if that's what it takes to save you.

Dear me,

I wish I could love you a little more, Not much, but at least a little more…

# Overripe Peaches

I tried to hold on to you, But it's time to let go.

I have clung long enough to your hands, It's time to let go –

I would've jumped out of skyscrapers

I would've built walls around so high to stop the sun from reaching us

But you left the phone unchecked

You slammed the door on my face.

You shut down into the depth of your shell while I waited,

I left my soul with you, and you gave me back tears,

I need to get out of us and start breathing.

We were two overripe peaches smashed together Couldn't say which was which

I waited for us to get over the pain of being with each other, I look at the whole of you now and see nothing.

Why is it that I am the one who is always giving? In the depth of my heart, I know I still love you

But love is not enough; it's not enough to make me stay.

# Graveyard of our Conversations

"We should never have met."You whisper in my ears.

It's true.

We should've been born as the sea and the beach with your waves all over me.

Taking a part of me with you

Every time you wash me.

"In my love, you drown."

We both know this is true. I loved, and I loved,

You started to drown in the ocean of my love Suffocated, all you wanted was to run away.

When I said I love you with all I got, you smiled

Choking, now you know what it means to be dead by love.

In the graveyard of our conversation, I stand,

I can see unfinished conversations flying like ghosts with no peace.

I can see the conversation where you first said, "I love you."

It rests in peace Conversations all around…

Some overtalked, some unfinished , I want to live within them;

Like a ghost, like the conversation, you always had in mind but never uttered.

# Dear Poem

All the words that bleed

All the memories that I spilled down on paper

All the people I killed

All the people I loved.

Dear poem,

Why are you staring at me in agony?

Is it because all I ever make you feel is pain and sorrow? Is it because I killed Mary and married Jo?

Is it because I cheated on Ross?

Is it because I loved Timothy and ran away from Susan? Is it me??

Dear poem, I'm sorry!

I longed to gift you sunlit walks through sunflower lanes,

Instead, I bathed you in blood and thrust your head into fire,

I'm sorry, I don't know otherwise!

All I ever knew was pain and chaos.

How could you, who come from me, be not agony but happiness?

# Kings and Kingfisher

Cigarette in your right hand The glass of beer on my left,
You never loved the sourness of beer nor I, the smell of cigarettes.

Our terrace had more cigarettes and beer bottles Than the old canal in the city,
Neither lilies or roses –
Our balcony; adorned with broken bottles and half-burnt cigarettes.

Kings and kingfishers; blended together in the perfect ratio
I got sick by your sadness, and you got drunk by my madness.

I took a puff; you took a drink,
Our eyes meet, without uttering a word, I kiss you.
 Smoke from your nose and soreness on my tongue,
I like the taste of you mixed with beer and cigarettes.

We are mad people, love!
People who broke the rehab, just to kiss –
I don't know why others make such a fuss…

We are mad people, love! People who took pain from love. I don't know how,
People who left each other just to miss – I don't know why
People who killed each other just to know how it feels to die.

# Was it today?

I ask myself, when did it begin to get so painful?

When did your heart start breaking for every little thing?

When did your chest and abdomen ache so badly whenever something bad happens?

When did you start to carve out scars for everything that hurts?

I look at myself in the mirror every day and ask, "When did you become so negative?"

When did that heart and body of yours break

For every little inconvenience in this bloody universe?

Was it today when you broke up with your lover?

Was it last month when a close friend of yours abandoned you?

Was it last year when the person you loved cheated on you?

Was it when a person you thought of as your guru masturbated with you in his mind?

Was it when you were touched where you shouldn't have been touched?

Was it when you were made to sit aside as a 6-year-old?

Was it when you were born?

Or was it the precise moment you began…as broken.

## Let Go

Want to step into the fire and burn,
Want to step into the water and drown;
Want to let go and stop breathing.

# **Runaway**

I don't wanna run away from who I am

I'm tired of running away from the storm

I can't see the sunrise from the horizon

It's been night in my head for years

I'm tired of filling this void with people You, me, and he, no one is enough

No one is ever enough. It's time to let go...

Let go of the pain, the heartbreaks, the emptiness, the anguish, the agony, the suffering...

What would it take for me to let go of all of it?

My pride? My courage? My voice?

If I am living, I live with this baggage Because there is comfort in this pain There is belonging in this agony

Something I never feel in anything or anyone.

Tell me, if time is what it takes, why is 23 years not enough to wash off these sins?

Do I need to kill myself to prove that I am living in pain?

Do I need to cut myself open to show you that inside me live demons and monsters?

I know that I don't deserve love

I know that I don't deserve the kindness I know it's tiring to just hold on to me

I don't want to stand in between you and your happiness.

If I don't leave now, you will leave when you know who I really am.

I know you love me, but spending time with me is like killing yourself You've already given me too much love

You got a choice now...

I don't want to wrap around your wholeness with my octopus hands, with my anxious love,

I love you to death, but you should run away when you have the time...

I'm done sabotaging love.

# How Much I Hate You

I am writing this to show how much I hate you.

The times when I thought what you had for me was love, I regret those days…

The times you put your hands around my body, Even if I never wanted to

I couldn't utter a word.

There were kisses all around my face.

I wanted none, I swear!

You made it look easy; you made it look like it was all my fault I couldn't utter a word .

I froze –

I wanted to run away from you, from the world, But all I could do was stand there;

Watch you do what you do to my body

I wanted to run away, from you, from this world.

The day you grabbed my breasts without even caring to ask

From that day, I was half dead

I have not yet been fully resurrected. I still live among the dead.

The shadows – they sometimes disappear and I sit alone in the darkness, Cursing myself for something you did

I'm done doing that!

I'm done blaming myself!

I want to say to myself that somewhere deep inside, there was love But something as pure as love cannot, will not be this

I want to hate you so much, but why is it that it is not possible? Deep inside, I want to forgive you for my own peace,

But why is it that it's not possible?

I'm done hating myself for the things you did to me.

I want to start loving me, at least stop all the noises inside my head

At least not get triggered when someone wants to passionately kiss me in dark spaces.

Why is it that I am still afraid, after all these months, after all these years?

Thinking, a shock of fear travels roundup my body.

I oughtn't to live my life like this, I want to forget you; forgiving is still hard…

Forget even the hate I have for you

I don't need the memory of you living inside my body

 I want to forget you, even if it means killing myself.

# Not Meant To Be

We're not meant to be
I know that; you know that
But when you kiss me on my lips
I can see the entire universe melting down
 I can see myself entering a black hole.


We're not meant to be
But when you whisper in my ears, "Say..." When we have nothing to say...
The silence doesn't put clutches on who I am Instead, I love them when you're with me
I love the serenity I love the noises
I love the dullest of things when I'm with you
I do the weirdest of things when you're in my mind.


We're not meant to be
I know that; you know that
But my darling, why is it that I want to love you more and more? Why is it that I crave your attention?
I would've missed you even if you had not walked into my life
Because sometimes it seems like you're the missing piece of the puzzle I've been searching for
 Sometimes you're just another stranger
"You're confused," you say. How can I not be
When I am feeling this kind of love for the first time?

How can I not be?

When you put your arms around me and kiss me? But you say, "We're not meant to be."

# Who Am I

I don't know who I am

Who I am when you take this negativity away from me. Empty mind and a scarred body.

I see no colors,

I see it all in black and white, I either hate or love,

I swing from high to low.

Cover my body with the blood of my own, Hang me from the horizon,

Tear out the negativity from my body. What will I do with the hole that's left?

Put your hands through the hollow abdomen

Feel the nothingness inside my body, inside my mind,

Say it's going to be okay and run away - when you have the time.

Before I name you a lover and hold you tight close to my chest Before I cling to you, run away from me –

Look at my face for one last time;

Tell me that you love me for the sake of it –

Run away before the whole of me wraps around the whole of you.

I bleed fire out of my scars, I kill the whole of me,

At least when I turn to ash, You will know I was human.

# Eulogy

Close your eyes and sit down; let me sing you a lullaby And put you to sleep –

A sleep from which you will never wake up

I will bring you wildflowers and a bottle of red wine

 I will shove my thoughts and write you a eulogy.

# Where does it go?

Lost love, unreturned and unseen,
Where does it dwell in nature's serene?
In shadows of night, with flowers it blends,
Its destination unknown, where affection transcends.

Within my closet, I seek to confine, Love's remnants lost,
 a tale so divine.
To suffocate, to drown, in its passionate wave,
The love I bled becomes the mark of my grave

# The Lady Next Door

The lady next door, I can hear her cry. I've been crying too
Every day and every night.
She tries to keep down her voice, I scream with all my vigor,
We both want to die.

I look through –
I don't see a difference, But she's 80, and I'm 20.

She has scars,
I've bleeding wounds; We both want to die.

She looks through with anger I let her feel the pain –
She is me,
And I decided not to die today.

# About the Author

**Irin Anna Cherian**

Irin Anna Cherian is a poet and scholar, currently pursuing her PhD in Economics at the prestigious Madras School of Economics. Her work has been featured in acclaimed anthologies such as Speaking Mirror and Inspirante series 2, where she has captivated readers with her ability to express deep, raw emotions. With a passion for turning the complexities of the human experience into verse, Cherian's writing delves into themes of love, pain, and resilience. Her vision is to craft poetry that resonates with readers on a visceral level, bringing the unspoken emotions of the heart to the forefront of every page

www.ingramcontent.com/pod-product-compliance
Lightning Source LLC
LaVergne TN
LVHW041641070526
838199LV00053B/3491